NEXT STOP, FREEDOM

The Story of a Slave Girl

Emily

NEXT STOP, FREEDOM

The Story of a Slave Girl

BY DOROTHY AND THOMAS HOOBLER

AND CAREY-GREENBERG ASSOCIATES

PICTURES BY CHERYL HANNA

SILVER BURDETT PRESS

Published by Silver Burdett Press, Inc.,
a division of Simon & Schuster, Inc.,
Prentice Hall Bldg.,
Englewood Cliffs, NJ 07632

Designed by Leslie Bauman

Illustrations on pages 51 and 53
by Leslie Dunlap

Manufactured in the United States of America

10 9 8 7 6 5 4 3 2 1

**Library of Congress Cataloging-
in-Publication Data**

Hoobler, Dorothy.
Next Stop, Freedom :
The story of a slave girl /
by Dorothy and Thomas Hoobler
and Carey-Greenberg Associates.
p.   cm.—(Her story)
Summary: Emily, a slave girl who
longs to read, escapes from slavery
with the help of Harriet Tubman.
[1. Slavery—Fiction.
2. Tubman, Harriet 1820?–1913—Fiction.
3. Afro-Americans—Fiction.]
I. Hoobler, Thomas.   II. Carey
-Greenberg Associates.
PZ7.H76227S1   1991
[Fic]—dc20   90-44361   CIP   AC
ISBN 0-382-24145-2 (lib. bdg.)
ISBN 0-382-24152-5

CONTENTS

Chapter One
"Why Can't I Learn to Read?"   *1*

Chapter Two
A Whipping   *11*

Chapter Three
Moses Is Coming!   *21*

Chapter Four
The Underground Railroad   *31*

Chapter Five
Road to Freedom   *40*

Making a Cornhusk Doll   *51*

CHAPTER ONE

"Why Can't I Learn to Read?"

BREAKFAST was bacon and eggs, and Emily was hungry. But she wasn't going to get any of it, not her. Cook had already given her a chunk of corn bread in the kitchen. That was all Emily would get unless somebody left a strip of bacon on his or her plate. Not likely.

The bacon and eggs were for Mas'r and Missus and their two sons, Frederick and Thomas. Emily had to stand by the big table while they ate, and brush the flies away with a turkey-feather whisk.

Because Emily was a slave.

She tried to remember the first time she knew that. Then the painful memory came back to her.

Her mamma, crying and wailing. Begging her master not to sell her children. But his heart was hard. Emily remembered looking back as the wagon took her and her brother away. Her mamma stood in the road and waved and called to them. Didn't make no difference.

If Mas'r felt like it, he could sell you, take you right out of the arms of your mamma. 'Cause you were a slave. That was why.

It was a little better because she had her brother, Isaiah, with her. Not so lonely as it would've been. Isaiah had been twelve, and Emily was six, when they got sold. That was four years ago.

When they got here, mas'r split them up right away. Isaiah went to live in the slave quarters and had to work in the fields. Emily was taken to the big house, where Mas'r and Missus lived.

Missus had wanted a little slave to watch over her two boys. Emily slept on a blanket on the floor of the nursery. Frederick and Thomas had been a pair of demons, even then. Emily had her hands full keeping them out of mischief.

"Emily! There's a fly on the table! Right there!" That was Thomas right now, the older boy, only two years younger than Emily.

Emily shook the whisk toward the fly. Thomas

looked up at her and grinned. He enjoyed bossing her around, just like his daddy, the Mas'r, bossed around everybody on the plantation. Except Missus.

Thomas was angry at Emily because yesterday she had stopped him from climbing out on the roof. He had called her all sorts of names, and then told her his father would whip her. But Missus heard all the commotion and came upstairs. She told Thomas that Emily was right, and he didn't like that one bit.

Mas'r and Missus finished their breakfast and left the table. Emily cleared away their plates and took them out to the kitchen. When she came back, Thomas was the only one there. She saw that his brother, Frederick, had left a slice of bacon on his plate.

Thomas saw her look at it. Before she could take the plate, he reached over and snatched the bacon. While she watched, he chewed it slowly. "Take these plates," he said. "Make sure you wash them clean." Emily glared at him, but kept her tongue to herself.

After she finished washing the dishes, Emily went upstairs. Today was Tuesday. That was the day the boys' teacher came to the plantation. They spent most of the day with him in the nursery, which was now a classroom. Emily always listened in unless Missus had something else for her to do.

When Emily arrived, Thomas was reading a book. The teacher was writing something on a slate for Frederick, who was just learning to read. Emily sat down on the floor. Next to her was the blue-backed book that children learned to read from.

She was curious. Reading always seemed a magical thing to her. Emily had listened when the teacher read stories to the boys. She knew he was getting them right out of the book. Downstairs in the library, the Mas'r had shelves and shelves of books. It made her head spin to think of all the stories they might have in them.

Emily picked up the blue-backed book, just to see what it looked like inside.

All of a sudden Thomas jumped up from his seat and knocked the book out of her hands. "Stop that!" he shouted.

Emily reached for the book, which had fallen to the floor, its pages crumpled. But Thomas stamped his foot to stop her. "Don't touch that! Slaves aren't allowed to read books," he said.

"I can't read," Emily said.

"You were trying to," said Thomas.

The teacher finally quieted him down, and sent Emily out of the room. In tears, she went downstairs and told Missus what had happened.

Missus frowned, as if Emily was at fault. "Go out to the quarters for the rest of the day," Missus said. "You can help Aunt Jen."

Emily made her way to the three log huts beyond the barn where the field slaves lived. The plantation was a small one, with only about two dozen slaves. Emily and Elva, the cook, were the only slaves who lived in the big house with Mas'r and his family.

All the field slaves would be working at this time of day, except for Aunt Jen. She was so old that the Mas'r didn't make her go in the fields any more. But she kept busy with a little garden where she grew turnips and peas and herbs.

Emily expected to see Aunt Jen out in her garden, but she wasn't there. Emily went inside one of the huts. She strained to see. The slave houses had no windows. There was a fireplace for cooking, but it wasn't lit during the day.

"Hush," Emily heard. It was Aunt Jen. She was in the corner of the cabin's one room. Emily saw that another slave was lying on a bed of straw there. Jen covered the slave with an old blanket and motioned Emily to go outside.

After a minute, Aunt Jen joined her. "That girl, Rachel, she's sure sick," Aunt Jen said. "I made her a cup of root tea, and now she's sleepin'. But her real trouble is she's just too weak for field work. Girl's only twelve, but she's as little and thin as you."

Emily hung her head. She had been all set to tell Aunt Jen about her own trouble, but that seemed too little to worry about now.

Aunt Jen was still talking. "Now if I could get some chicken broth and a little meat into her, it would help. You think Cook would send some for her?"

"Aunt Jen, I don't even get to eat chicken, unless somebody leaves a scrap on his plate. Missus is awful careful about the food. And Cook is afraid of her."

Aunt Jen just shook her head. "We'll just have to trust the Lord will bring her through. What brings you down here? Thought those two boys kept you busy enough."

"Missus told me to come down here because the boys' teacher is here today. That Thomas is acting awful mean to me lately," she said.

"He sees his papa order the slaves around. That's what he feels like doin' to you. Makes him feel big." Aunt Jen sat down in the shade next to the house. "Let's make us some cornhusk dolls. We'll call one of them Thomas." She laughed softly. "Treat him any way we like."

Aunt Jen took a handful of the dried husks of corn that lay on the ground. She could make hats, dolls, and lots of other things out of them. Emily watched Aunt Jen's wrinkled, bony hands. They moved as swiftly as if they had eyes of their own.

"How'd you learn to do that?" Emily asked suddenly.

"Do this?" Aunt Jen held out the doll, which she had tied at the top to make a head. "Oh, my, I guess I watched somebody do it, just the way you watchin' me."

"You didn't learn it out of a book?"

"Book?" Aunt Jen looked at Emily. "You know slaves can't read." But she had a twinkle in her eye when she said it.

Emily began to cry. "That's what Thomas said." She explained what happened in the classroom. "Can't slaves learn to read, Aunt Jen?"

Jen laughed again. "Course they can." She drew a squiggly line in the dust with her finger. "See that? That's an *S*, and it makes a noise just like this: *ssss*. You remember a noise a snake makes when it's trapped? That's an *S* noise. You see an *S* in a book, that's what it means."

Emily looked. She drew an *S* in the dust. It wasn't hard at all! "Show me some more."

"Well, here's a little circle. That's an easy one—that's an *O*. Watch my mouth. See it make a circle? Say it now, child: *ooooo*."

Emily was excited. "But that's not hard, Auntie. I can learn that."

"Sure you can."

"But why do they say slaves can't read?"

"Why, child, the whites are all afraid that if the slaves learn to read, they'll get too smart. Then they'll figure out they're just as good as the whites."

"Then they won't be slaves?"

Aunt Jen shook her head. "No, child. They'll still be slaves."

"But why, Aunt Jen? Why are we slaves?"

Jen brushed herself off and stood up. She handed the doll to Emily. "See this?" she said. "Now it's yours. You can do what you like with it. That's us slaves. Somebody sold us to the white people, and they treat us however they want. That's just the way it is."

"But we're not dolls! We're people."

"Don't make no difference a'tall. I'm tired now. You want to help me a little? Go out and take some of those weeds out of my garden. I'm goin' inside to sit with little Rachel."

Emily did as she was told. But all the time she was working, she kept thinking about the *S* and the *O*. And that night, after the boys were asleep, she sneaked back into the classroom again.

Moonlight was shining through the window, making it easy for her to see. She sat there, silently turning the pages of the little blue-backed book. There were a lot more letters to learn. But some of them had pictures next to them to help you figure them out. It might take her a long time, but Emily promised herself that she would learn what they all meant. Slaves could read. They could!

CHAPTER TWO

A Whipping

MAS'R WASN'T at the table for breakfast. Emily thought he must have gone on a trip. But Thomas kept looking at her as if he knew a secret.

Right afterward, Missus came out to the kitchen and told Emily and the cook that they had to come outside.

All the other slaves were gathered in a group in the farmyard. Mas'r was already there, giving a speech. He was talking about stealing and how wrong it was. He sounded like the white preachers that held services for the slaves on Sundays. But Mas'r seemed very angry.

Emily heard one of the slaves whisper to Cook, "There was a chicken missing from the coop this morning. Some fool took it for that sick gal." Emily's spine tingled. She looked around, wondering if Aunt Jen had done it. But no, she was sitting by the cabin, just like always.

Then two slaves came out from the barn, dragging a third slave between them. Emily cried out, and somebody put a hand over her mouth.

The third slave, with his arms held behind him, was her brother, Isaiah! Emily's knees turned to jelly. She wanted to run away because she knew what was going to happen. But she couldn't move.

The plantation's overseer, Yardley, followed the slaves from the barn. He was carrying his whip.

Everybody was afraid of Yardley. His job was to keep the field slaves working all day. Emily didn't see him much, but she heard the other slaves talk about him. He hardly ever spoke. But if you thought he wasn't looking and stopped to rest, right away you felt the crack of Yardley's whip.

Yardley was smiling now, showing his dirty teeth. Slaves said Mas'r kept Yardley around because he did things Mas'r wasn't cruel enough to do. Yardley liked doing them.

The slaves dragged Isaiah up in front of Mas'r. Mas'r said in a voice everybody could hear, "Now, you know stealing is wrong, don't you?"

Isaiah said nothing. This seemed to make Mas'r more angry. "I can't abide a thief on my plantation. You have to be punished. You understand that?"

Still Isaiah didn't speak. Mas'r said something to Yardley. Yardley ordered the slaves to tie Isaiah to a big tree, with his arms around the trunk. Yardley uncoiled the big black whip that he carried.

Emily shut her eyes. She couldn't bear to see what would happen next. But when she heard the loud *crack!* of the whip, she winced as if she herself had been struck. All around her the slaves moaned softly.

No one spoke. The yard was silent. Then came the *crack!* a second time, and a third. Emily couldn't stand it. She wanted to run away. *Tell him!* she thought fiercely, wishing she could shout it at her brother. *Tell him you're sorry!*

But there was no sound until the *crack!* came again. Emily's eyes filled with tears, and she had to open them. Dimly she saw the big red welts across her brother's back. She felt them as deeply as if they had been on her own body.

Yardley looked as determined as if he was chopping wood. Each time his whip came down, Isaiah's body seemed to tremble. But Isaiah still wouldn't speak. Finally, his knees buckled. His body slumped down, with only the ropes holding him to the tree.

Yardley raised his whip again, but Mas'r stepped forward and caught his arm. "That's enough," Mas'r said. "Leave him there."

Yardley looked disappointed. Then he turned and saw all the slaves looking at him. He cracked the whip in their direction. "Time to work!" he shouted. "Sun's high in the sky. You lazy devils'll work double fast today to make up for the time you've lost."

Quickly the crowd broke up. The slaves moved toward the cotton fields beyond the barn. Only Emily and Cook were left. Cook took Emily's shoulders and turned her away. "Don't say nothing," Cook said. "Nothing you can do now. You can visit him later."

Emily cried softly as they walked back to the big house. Cook led her inside the kitchen. "I know it's hard for you," she said to Emily. "But every time I see a whipping I tell myself how lucky I am. I get to live here in the big house. I don't have to go down in the fields with that

Yardley standing over me. You remember that too."

Emily shook her head.

"Go on, now," Cook said. "Ask Missus what she's got for you today. Just like nothing happened."

Emily stumbled through the house to the sitting room. Missus was there with the boys. When Missus looked up, Emily thought she saw a touch of concern in her eyes. But then she caught sight of Thomas and the nasty smile he gave her. Emily's back stiffened. She blinked back her tears. She would never let him see her cry. Never!

"The boys want to ride their ponies today," Missus said. "Go down and get them out of the barn."

All day Emily went through her duties, trying not to think about the whipping. She didn't say anything to Thomas unless she had to. But at supper, when she was taking his empty plate from the table, he jolted her arm. She dropped the plate, and it smashed on the floor.

"Look at that!" Thomas said. He turned to Emily, "If you're not careful, my father will whip you."

"That's enough, Thomas," Missus said.

Emily knelt and picked up the pieces of the plate. She carried it out to the kitchen and waited until the door closed behind her before she cried.

"Here, now," Cook said. "I'll take care of the rest of the plates. Take this pot of grease down to Aunt Jen. She'll know what to do with it."

Relieved, Emily ran out the door with the grease. No matter what Cook said, it was terrible to live in that house. Then she stopped. She reminded herself that she wanted to learn to read. She had to stay in the house to do that. Someday she would be able to read all the books in the big house. Then she'd see what Thomas had to say.

Emily made her way to Aunt Jen's cabin. Isaiah was inside. He sat on a bed of straw with a flannel blanket over his shoulders. He stared at Emily. There was a look in his eyes that she had never seen before. Not fear. Something else. He had always been so jolly, telling jokes and laughing. Now he was sad in a way that seemed like he'd never be happy again.

Emily turned away. She didn't want her brother to know she had seen him whipped.

Aunt Jen took the pot of grease from her.

"That's my good Emily," she said. "Lie down, now," Aunt Jen told Isaiah. "We'll smear this on, and you won't feel those stripes."

"I'll always feel them," Isaiah said, but he did what she told him. Aunt Jen showed Emily how to work the grease into his wounds.

When she had finished, Isaiah sat up again. He looked at Emily. "I'm running away," he said. "I'll never work for Mas'r again."

"Now hush that foolish talk," Aunt Jen said. "Where you going to go? That Yardley will get out the dogs and be after you straight away. You don't stand a chance."

"I'll follow the star," Isaiah said. "To freedom." He looked at Emily. "You coming with me?"

"No, no, now she's not," Aunt Jen said. "You lie down and let those wounds heal."

She hustled Emily outside. "Don't listen to him," Aunt Jen said. "He'll get over that. He's a smart young fella. His pride is hurt, is all."

"What did he mean, he'd follow the star?" asked Emily.

Aunt Jen chuckled. "I thought all the slaves knew about the star," she said. She pointed up into the dark sky. "See that bright star right about there? All by itself. Just a little above the trees?"

Emily looked and saw the twinkling star Aunt Jen was pointing to. It seemed brighter than all the rest of the stars.

"That's called the North Star," said Aunt Jen. "Folks say if you keep that star above you as you walk, you'll get to the North. No slaves there, they say. Everybody's free!"

"Oh!" Emily said. "I'd be free?"

"Maybe," Aunt Jen said. "But it's a long, long way. You might as well try to walk to the stars themselves. If Yardley didn't find you with his dogs, the paddyrollers would."

"Who are they?"

"Paddyrollers, child? They's people who hunt down escaped slaves. You know you got to have a pass to leave the plantation, don't you? Well, the paddyrollers ride all night looking for slaves without a pass. They get a reward for bringing you back."

"But maybe they wouldn't find you," said Emily.

"Naw, they would, child. And I seen what happens to them that tries to run away. Worse than what happened to your brother. I'll talk him out of it. No use thinking about running away."

But as Emily walked back to the big house, that was all she thought about. She looked at the star. Freedom! What would it be like to be free?

CHAPTER THREE

Moses Is Coming!

SUNDAY CAME at last. It was the one day of the week that the slaves didn't have to work. This Sunday they were going on a trip to a nearby plantation. A preacher was visiting, and Mas'r thought it was a good idea for them to hear him. Mas'r gave each of them a pass, and they started walking down the road in a group.

Emily saw her brother walking with Aunt Jen. He hadn't run away, and she was glad. She would have felt lonely without him. She ran to catch up with them. She put her hand in her brother's. But he just stared ahead, hardly seeming to notice her.

Emily showed her pass to Aunt Jen. "Is my name on here, Aunt Jen?" Emily asked.

"No, child, it says, 'This slave can pass on the roads until nightfall Sunday.' Then Mas'r wrote his own name, so they know who you belong to."

"I wish he'd written my name. I'd like to see it written out just once."

"Keep studyin', child, and you can do it yourself."

"I sneak into the schoolroom 'most every night," Emily said. "I can figure out a lot of letters, but it's tricky putting them together. My name's got an *M* and an *L,* and I think one or two *E*s."

"See there? You're catchin' on, as good as those two boys, I bet."

Suddenly, those who were in front of the group stopped. One of them looked around, and Emily did too. Nobody else was in sight. It was quiet except for the birds singing. The first slave waved his arm and walked into the woods alongside the road. Everyone followed. Aunt Jen tugged Emily along.

"This isn't the right way," Emily said.

"We're goin' to hear a preacher," Aunt Jen said.

"Not that white preacher," another slave said. "One of our own."

Emily was puzzled. "How do we know where to find him?"

"There's a special place," Aunt Jen said, patting her hand. "I been there before. We just got to get back before nightfall. Nobody'll miss us."

Pretty soon, they came to a clearing in the woods. A lot of other slaves were already there. Everybody seemed excited. A woman stood up and started to sing, and other voices joined in:

> The big bee flies high,
> The little bee makes the honey.
> The black folks make the cotton
> And the white folks get the money.

Everybody laughed and clapped.

All at once they were silent. A black man in a black suit stepped into the clearing. Emily was surprised to see that he carried a book.

People began to sit down. Emily found a place between her brother and Aunt Jen.

The preacher began to speak. His voice was deep and seemed to fill the forest. "This here's the Bible, and I'm going to read you a story that the other preachers don't tell. It's about Moses."

Some of the other slaves called out, "Moses!"

The preacher opened the book. It was true— slaves could read! He read them the story of Moses. Emily sat fascinated. Moses' people had been slaves too, in some place called Egypt. But they wanted to be free!

And everybody repeated the word, "Free! Yes!"

God showed Moses the way, and he led his people out of Egypt. But the pharaoh chased them.

Emily was excited. She wanted them to get away, but she was afraid they'd be caught. And they almost were. They came to a big sea, like a river, and couldn't get across.

"Save them, Lord!" a woman called.

And He did. The waters opened up, and Moses led his people across. And then, when the pharaoh's men rode into the river, it closed up again!

Everybody cheered.

The preacher closed his book. "That's what it really says in the Bible. No man can keep another in slavery."

An old man called out, "My master kept me now for sixty years. Every day of my life I worked for him, and he sold my wife and children!"

"Yes," the preacher said. "The white preachers tell you that the Bible says you shall not steal.

And that is so. But your masters have been steal-ing from you for years. They steal your work. They steal your children. They steal your lives."

He shook his finger at them. "But Moses is coming."

The slaves cheered. The woman who had sung before stood up now and began a new song. The clearing was filled with the sound:

> Go down, Moses
> Way down in Egypt land
> Tell old pharaoh
> Let my people go.

They sang verse after verse. After that, the meeting broke up. The slaves went back to their own plantations.

Sunday dinner was the best meal of the week. Before they had left, the slaves had buried pota-toes in a bed of hot ashes. When they were dug up, they were toasted clean through. Mas'r let them have some side meat—fat pork—and they cooked it slowly over an open fire till it was crispy. Cook was allowed to make real biscuits in the big house's oven for the slaves. There were plenty of turnips and boiled greens too. Aunt Jen said eating greens was what kept her strong.

They all sat down outside the slave quarters to enjoy the meal. People sang "Go Down, Moses" one more time. Emily saw that even Isaiah joined in.

"Is Moses really coming for us?" Emily asked Aunt Jen.

Jen just smiled. "Makes you feel good to think she is, don't it? I been hearing that tale all my life."

"I thought Moses was a man," Emily said.

"Not our Moses," a woman said.

The other slaves began to talk about Moses. "Sometimes she disguises herself," said one. "Moses wears men's clothes and rides a big black horse."

"Naw," said another, "she runs through the woods faster'n any horse."

"I heard she fought a big old overseer with her fists and beat him."

"Like to see her take on Yardley."

They all laughed.

"They sent dogs after her one time, and she caught 'em and ate 'em."

"She goes wherever she pleases, and no pad-dyroller ever finds her."

Emily's eyes were wide. "Is that right, Aunt Jen?"

"Well, child, they tell a lot of stories about Moses. She comes to take the slaves to freedom, so they say. I heard she'd been close by lots of times, but I ain't never seen her."

Jen hesitated and looked around. She lowered her voice. "Funny things begin to happen when folks hear Moses is comin'."

"What kinds of things?"

Jen shook her head. "You just make sure you're in your bed where you're supposed to be tonight."

Emily saw Isaiah whispering with some of the others. She went over to him.

"Isaiah, are you going to run away?"

"If Moses comes," he said.

"You won't leave me behind, will you?" she said.

He squeezed her hand and winked. Almost, but not quite, he smiled.

When it got dark, Emily went back to the big house. She saw to it that the boys got into bed. Then she lay down on her blanket on the floor of the boys' bedroom. Soon they were snoring, but she couldn't sleep. She kept thinking of the stories the slaves had told about Moses.

But she must have dozed off, for the next thing she knew the fire bell was ringing. She smelled smoke coming through the window.

Instantly she got up. If there was a fire, she had to get the children out of the house. Thomas was already stirring. "Get outside!" Emily shouted. He ran out the door, leaving Emily to bring Frederick.

When Emily brought Frederick outside into the yard, she could see the flames. They flickered up over the roof of the stables.

"My pony!" Frederick cried. He wanted to run down there, but she held him back. She saw Yardley and the Mas'r run by.

Soon, all the slaves were out of their cabins. They carried water in buckets from the pump toward the stables. Everybody was shouting. Mas'r soon appeared, leading two of the horses behind him. Then he went back for more.

Missus took Frederick from Emily and tried to get him to come inside the house. But he was still worried about his pony. So Missus asked Emily to go down to the stables to see if the ponies got out.

People were running every which way. The smoke kept her from seeing much, but when the stables collapsed, there was a big whoosh of flame. Suddenly, Emily saw a boy with the ponies. His face was all black, and she thought it was a slave. But as he came closer, she saw it was Thomas with his face smeared with soot. She

laughed, and then clapped her hand over her mouth. He had heard her. He shot her a look of pure hatred, but gave her the ponies to hold. Then he ran back toward the fire.

Emily led the ponies back to the house. When Frederick saw them, he clapped his hands. "Thank you, Emily," Missus said.

Emily went back to the stables to see if there was anything else she could do. But by now everybody was just standing around watching. The fire was almost out, but the stables were destroyed.

Behind her Emily heard someone say, "It was Moses." She turned. It was Rachel, the girl who had been sick. Her eyes were white, staring at the wreckage. "Moses set the fire," she whispered to Emily.

CHAPTER FOUR

The Underground Railroad

OF COURSE, Thomas tried to blame Emily. He told how she laughed when she saw him with the ponies. But Missus said Emily must have been nervous, that's all. She was grateful that Emily had taken Frederick out of the house and brought his pony to him. Mas'r was too busy planning to build new stables to bother with what Thomas said.

Mas'r took some of the slaves from the fields to work on the stables. It was the busiest time of the year too. Cotton was ready to be picked. Yardley just worked the slaves even harder to get the work done.

But things went on happening, just like Aunt

Jen said they would. The morning after the fire, Cook told Missus that there were no eggs for breakfast. When Cook had gone to the hen house, not a single egg was to be found. "The hens must have been frightened by the fire," Missus said. Cook just nodded, but when she was alone with Emily, she said, "I bet Moses took them eggs."

Work on the stables went slowly. There were a lot of accidents. One whole wall fell down almost as soon as it was finished. Mas'r was real angry. He told Missus that the slaves didn't know enough to nail boards together right. But out in the yard Emily heard one of the workers say, "Moses must 'a pushed that wall over."

Even Yardley was having trouble. When he was riding across the fields, his horse suddenly shied and threw him. The horse ran away, and the slaves had to spend most of the day looking for him. Emily helped too, and heard that Moses had put a big old rattlesnake right under the horse's hooves.

She got the idea after that. Next morning, she was putting the sugar and salt out for breakfast. All at once she got them mixed up. And sure enough, when Mas'r took a sip of his coffee, he nearly choked.

Then Emily made a big mistake. She couldn't stop herself from laughing. When everyone looked at her, she said, "Moses must 'a done it."

Mas'r didn't believe that for some reason. But he wouldn't listen when Thomas wanted to have Emily whipped. Instead he told her she had to work for a week in the fields. "When you come back," he said, "you'll know how lucky you are to work in my house."

That was true enough, though she didn't know it at the time. She was relieved, in a way, not to have to take care of Thomas and Frederick. But she never had known how hard field work could be.

Yardley grinned when he gave her a big burlap sack. "You got to fill this," he said. "I weigh all the sacks at the end of the day. If you don't pick twenty pounds' worth, back out you go."

Emily had no idea how much twenty pounds was, but she started out. She had to stoop over each time she saw a cotton boll to pick. Then she had to pull it off, and not hurt the plant either. Put it in her sack, and then go on up the row. The one time she stopped to rest, *crack!* came Yardley's whip. She jumped. He hadn't hit her, but she started working fast again.

The slaves stopped to eat at noon. By then

Emily's dress was soaked with sweat. Her fingers were raw, and her back ached terribly. She rushed to the water barrel and dipped the big ladle into it. Isaiah put his hand on her arm. "Careful," he said. "Don't drink it fast, or you'll get an awful bellyache."

"And that won't get you outa work either," an older woman said.

Emily shared the hoecakes that the slaves made from flour and water. They baked them on the blades of hoes, held over a fire. It had almost no taste, but she was eager for anything that would fill her stomach.

"Old hog round the bend," one of the slaves said, and everyone got up. That was a signal that meant Yardley was coming. It was time to go back to the fields.

Emily didn't think she was going to last. Her knees felt weak, and she began to kneel to pick the cotton. That saved her back, but getting back up was hard. And Yardley was everywhere with his whip. She forced herself to go on, just to spite him.

Isaiah worked his way over to Emily's row. When Yardley's back was turned, he dumped some of the cotton bolls out of his sack. "Take these," he said. "You're not near finished."

Emily looked up. The sun was starting to go

down. She lifted her bag. It was only half full. She tried to work harder, but it was all she could do just to stay on her feet.

Finally, Yardley started to move the slaves toward the barn. Emily was last to come in, dragging her sack behind her.

The slaves formed a line, and Yardley was at the front, weighing the bags. He couldn't see Emily from where he was, and the other slaves started to pass cotton back to her. She slipped them inside her bag. Isaiah was next to her. He lifted Emily's bag and shook his head.

Checking to see that Yardley was still busy, Isaiah picked up a couple of rocks. He put them into the bag and shook it so they fell to the bottom. "He might find them later," Isaiah said. "But he doesn't always check."

When it was Emily's turn to have her bag weighed, she held her breath. Yardley put it on the scales. She looked at his face. He scowled. "Just made it," he sneered. "I told Mas'r I could make you straighten out. You'll do more tomorrow."

Emily followed the others back to the slave quarters. Aunt Jen had a pot of greens on the boil. Emily collapsed on the ground. "I just got to sleep, Aunt Jen," she said. "I can't eat."

"Child, the best thing for you is greens and

some of that pot liquor. I put some pig feet inside the pot."

It did smell awful good, and Emily had some of it. But right after, she went inside Aunt Jen's cabin and fell asleep in a corner.

She dreamed of Yardley though. He kept chasing her, and all of a sudden she woke up. Yardley had caught her! She struggled, but a strong arm held her tight.

"Hush, gal." It was a voice she didn't know. "Your brother told me you was ready to be free."

Another voice came out of the darkness— Aunt Jen's. "It's Moses, Emily. Sure's you born, Moses has come to free you."

Emily got up and went outside. In the moonlight she could see the other slaves from the cabins. Isaiah ran up and hugged her. "We're going to be free," he said.

Suddenly, Emily thought of something. "Wait," she said, "I've got to go back to the big house."

"Cook don't want to go," said Isaiah.

"It's not that."

Moses heard her. "Can't wait, girl," she said. "The Underground Railroad is pullin' out."

"What's that?" Emily said.

"That's my railroad, and we're leavin'."

"I'll catch up with you," Emily said. She pulled away from Isaiah and ran for the house.

All the windows were dark. The house looked spooky in the moonlight, and Emily was frightened as she slipped in the back door. But she could find her way around, even in the dark.

The staircase to the second floor creaked as she stepped on it. The sound seemed as loud as an alarm bell, and she stopped, trying not to breathe.

She couldn't hear anything, and she went on up. She slipped by the boys' bedroom and heard them snoring. Right next to it was the nursery. She went inside and right away found what she was looking for. The blue-backed book. As she picked it up, she saw Thomas's slate next to it.

Her hand was shaking, but she picked up the chalk. She had never written anything before, except practicing with her finger in the dust. She wrote an *E* on the slate. She held it up in the moonlight. It was just like the *E* in the book. Now Thomas would know—know that slaves could read.

Quick as a dragonfly on water, she slipped out the door, down the stairs, and outside. Aunt Jen was waiting there for her. "Hurry, child," Jen said. "They went up the creek."

"Aren't you coming?" Emily said.

"Land no. I'm too old. I'd just hold you all back and be trouble. It's enough for me just to see Moses and know that she's real. 'Sides, I don't want to miss the look on Yardley's face tomorrow."

"Oh, Aunt Jen, I'll never forget you."

"You better not. And I'll remember you too. I see what you took there. I thought that's what it was. Don't forget your dream. Go on, now. Scat!"

Emily ran, faster than she ever had in her life. She reached the creek and followed it into the woods.

It was dark here. The trees hid the moon, and she could barely see. She heard an owl hoot, and stopped. The old slaves said that someone was dying when they heard an owl. She shook her head to put that thought away. She stepped into the shallow creek. In the darkness it was the only way she could follow it.

It wasn't much harder to run here, she thought. Then she tripped over a rock and sprawled into the water.

The book! She mustn't lose it. She felt around with her hands and found it. Just then, somebody grabbed her from behind.

CHAPTER FIVE

Road to Freedom

EMILY SCREAMED, and her head was pushed down under the water.

She struggled, and whoever held her pulled her back up. He had the strongest arms Emily had ever felt.

"You're one of the most troublesome people I ever took on my railroad." It wasn't a man. It was Moses. "You gonna bring every paddyroller in the county down on us."

"I'm sorry," Emily said. "I'll be real quiet, honest I will." She looked around. "Where are the others?"

"On up the stream. I heard you coming and thought I better get you on board. Or drown you. Now follow me. Step where I step."

Emily did as she was told. Moses was a short, heavy woman, but she moved like a deer. She didn't make any more noise than the water running over the rocks.

But she didn't seem to walk straight. First she walked up the creek, then stepped out and moved along the bank for a while. Then back across to the other side of the stream. Emily had to pay close attention, for she didn't know where they were going next.

Finally, they caught up with the others. Moses lifted her head and sniffed. "Trouble," she said. Emily sniffed, but she couldn't smell anything but sweet honeysuckle flowers.

Moses moved faster now. She led them away from the stream. It was hard for Emily to keep up, and it seemed like they were moving in circles. "We come by this spot before," she heard someone whisper.

Moses shushed them with a sound like a dog growling. Then they heard another sound: a pack of hounds barking, somewhere far behind them.

The slaves hurried on. Sometimes the dogs seemed nearer. Then the sound of their barking drifted away, only to reappear again. Soon it was very close.

Moses stopped. They were on the edge of the woods. A field of corn stood in front of them. The stalks were high, above their heads. "Go in there," she said to the others. "Get far inside and wait for me." Then she ran back in the direction of the barking.

Emily followed the others. They moved into the field, and the corn closed around them. They sat down and listened as the dogs came nearer and nearer. "We got to run," said one man. "No," the others told him. "Moses said to wait."

Emily hunched her shoulders and clutched her book to her chest. She had once seen a fox that Yardley's dogs had attacked at the chicken coop. She shut her eyes tight, trying not to see it now.

Then the dogs' barking moved in the other direction. A shot rang out, and everyone gasped. A woman began to moan softly. Someone shushed her. "Moses can't die."

Gradually the sound of the barking died away. Now they could hear nothing but each other breathing. They waited a long time. Emily's head nodded. She could hear some of the others snoring.

All at once Moses was next to her. Emily jumped. She hadn't heard a thing, not even the cornstalks brushing together. "Are you all right?" Emily said.

"Sure 'nough," Moses said. "I took them dogs back to where we crossed our track. They got all confused and went back down the creek again." She yawned. "We'll stay here and see where we are tomorrow." She leaned against Emily, and quick as that, she was asleep.

In the morning they found that the corn was ripe, and that was their breakfast. Moses took Isaiah and a couple of the men and went off for a little while. When they came back, they were carrying hoes and scythes. "Everyone take one of these," Moses said. "We'll look like we're going off to work."

They started off down a little dirt road, right out in the open. Emily could see Moses clearly for the first time. She had a nasty scar on the side of her forehead. Emily was embarrassed when Moses caught her staring.

Moses said, "Got that a long time ago. Stopped a mean overseer from catching a slave who was escaping. He clubbed me right across the face." She grinned, showing a big gap between her teeth. "Knocked out my two front teeth too."

"When do we come to the railroad?" Emily asked.

Moses laughed. "We're on the railroad right now. That's just a name the slave masters gave it. When slaves escape, and the paddyrollers can't find them, they say they must 'a gone underground. But it's real enough. All through the South there's places to hide or get some help. Those are the stations on the Underground Railroad."

"How do you know where they are?" asked Emily.

"You learn the way. When I ran away from my master, I was lucky. I found a family whose house was a stop on the railroad. They took me to the next safe place. Finally, I got to Pennsylvania."

"Is that in the North? Are slaves really free there?"

"Sure 'nough. No slaves there. We got our own church and school, our own houses, and get paid for our work."

Emily thought about this. It seemed like a dream. Suddenly Moses put up her hand. "Hold up!" she said. "Horse comin'." Emily listened, but it was another few seconds before she could faintly hear the hoofbeats.

Moses led them into the trees alongside the road. As they watched, a wagon came into sight, carrying a big load of hay. A black man was driving it. Moses ran out into the road. "Halt!" she cried. Surprised, the man reined in the horse.

"Where you takin' that hay?" she said.

"On into town."

"What town's that?"

"Clayton."

"You got a pass?"

The man reached for his pocket and then stopped. "I don't got to show my pass to you."

"Don't you know who I am?"

The man looked at her. "Oh, glory!" he said. "You's Moses! The paddyrollers was at our place this mornin'. They're all around here lookin' for you."

"You got passengers," she said, and whistled through the gap in her teeth. Emily and the rest stepped out of the woods.

"Oh, glory," the man said.

They burrowed into the hay, hiding from sight, and the wagon continued on down the road. A few minutes later, Emily heard more hoofbeats—a lot of them. The wagon stopped, and she could hear a gruff voice ask the man for his pass. There was a long silence, and then: "You see any slaves along this road?"

"I did, yassuh. A whole lot of 'em, back about

a mile. They ran in the woods when they saw me comin'."

"Let's go!" The hoofbeats clattered off in the other direction, and the wagon started up again.

Moses whispered to Emily. "See now? That's how the railroad works."

Later, the wagon stopped again. "We're comin' to town," the driver said.

"Time to change trains," Moses said. They wiggled out of the hay. "You want to come to freedom with us?" Moses said to the driver.

He hesitated. "I got a wife and three kids. Mas'r will treat them bad if I run off."

"Who's your master?"

"Mr. Davis."

"All right. I'll be back in the spring sometime. I'll find you all then."

Moses led them across a field. "Do you really come back all the time?" Emily asked her.

"Oh, I took more trips back South than I can count."

"But what if they catch you?"

"They sure want to. But as long as three million of our people are slaves, there's work for me to do. And I got lots of helpers." She pointed to the other side of the field.

Emily saw a big farmhouse. A white girl was

feeding chickens in the yard. She wore a gray dress and sunbonnet. As they drew nearer, she looked up and saw them. She called toward the house.

"Shouldn't we hide?" Emily asked. Moses took her hand. "These are Friends," she said. "A Quaker family. They hate slavery as much as we do."

A man in a black vest and broad-brimmed hat came out of the house. He clasped Moses' hand. "Harriet Tubman," he said. "Thee are welcome, as always."

Harriet—for that was her real name—and the slaves stayed with the Quakers for a week. There was a secret room in their cellar to hide the passengers on the Underground Railroad.

During the day they had to stay indoors, but Emily made herself useful around the kitchen. Hannah, who had been feeding the chickens when they first arrived, was the same age as Emily. "I see thee always keeps thy book with you," she said.

Emily felt her face get hot. "I want to learn to read someday," she said.

"I can read," said Hannah. "Let us open thy book together."

Hannah gave Emily a slate to write on. One by

one, Emily learned how to make all the letters. Carefully, she put together the letters of her name: EMILY. As she looked at it, tears came to her eyes.

Hannah smiled. "Thee must write me a letter from Philadelphia."

"I promise," said Emily. "And I'll be back too. When I'm older, I'm going to help Moses. I'm going to find my mother and make her free."

The day came for them to leave. The paddy-rollers had given up trying to find them. Another Quaker had brought a wagon to take Emily, Isaiah, and the others to Pennsylvania.

Moses hugged Emily. "Aren't you going?" Emily asked.

"No, there's more work for me to do," she said. "Have to keep the railroad running. Climb aboard now. The next stop is freedom."

Emily got onto the wagon, and it started off. She remembered the time she had seen her mother crying in the road. She looked back, wanting to wave to Moses. But she was already gone, keeping the railroad running, running through the night.

MAKING A
CORNHUSK DOLL

CHILDREN in many times and places have enjoyed playing with dolls. Some archeologists think dolls are the oldest form of toys. Dolls were buried in children's graves as long as 5,000 years ago in Egypt. In ancient Greece and Rome, girls took their dolls to the temple of Venus or Diana to show that they were ready to marry.

The cornhusk dolls were first made by Native Americans (who were also the first to grow corn as food). They decorated their dolls with feathers, beadwork, shells, and skins. Slaves had made their own dolls in Africa, from such materials as raffia (string) and millet stalks. They soon adopted the doll-making materials they found in America.

Materials Needed

Cornhusks, String, Scissors, Warm water, Sponge, Pipe cleaners, White glue, Scraps of cloth.

Steps

1. Trim the tips and stem ends off the cornhusk leaves to make straight edges at either end.
2. If husks are dry, soak them in water so that they will bend without breaking. As you work, continue to keep them moist with a sponge.
3. Put six husks together in a bundle, with the smooth sides turned outward. Tie the bundle in the middle with string.
4. Turn down the husks above the string. Peel each one down the way you peel a banana.
5. Tie the bundle again, this time about an inch from the top. This forms the head of the doll.
6. Take another husk and roll it around a pipe cleaner. Tie the ends and the center. This will be the arms of the doll.

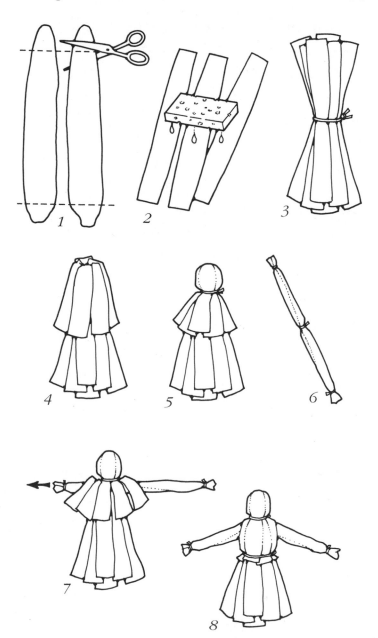

7. Push the arm piece under the turned-down husks below the head. Hold it there while you do the next step.

8. Roll up another husk and tuck it under the arms. Tie a string below it to form the waist of the doll. The basic doll is now complete. You can add any of the following steps:

9. Drape a husk over the shoulders and tie it at the waist to form a shawl.

10. Tie more husks at the waist and turn them down to make a fuller skirt.

11. Bend the arms in any position.

12. Accessories such as a bonnet or purse can be formed from more husks. Ribbons or scraps of cloth can be added as decorations.

Tips

When you have fresh corn, save the inner leaves. They will be smoother and better for making the doll. Dry them on a sheet of newspaper. Keep them flat by placing another sheet of newspaper and a heavy book on top.

Seeds can be glued to the face to make eyes, nose, and mouth.

Another kind of doll can be made by dividing the husks below the waist into two sections. Pipe cleaners tied inside each of the two sections will make legs for the doll.